To Mo, my lifelong friend —J. L.

For Por Por, from your number-four grandchild! —O. C. M.

STERLING CHILDREN'S BOOKS
New York

An Imprint of Sterling Publishing Co., Inc.
1166 Avenue of the Americas
New York, NY 10036

ISBN 978-1-4549-2739-6

Distributed in Canada by Sterling Publishing Co., Inc.
C/o Canadian Manda Group, 664 Annette Street
Toronto, Ontario M6S 2C8, Canada
Distributed in the United Kingdom by GMC Distribution Services
Castle Place, 166 High Street, Lewes, East Sussex BN7 1XU, England
Distributed in Australia by NewSouth Books
45 Beach Street, Coogee, NSW 2034, Australia

For information about custom editions, special sales, and premium and corporate purchases,
please contact Sterling Special Sales at 800-805-5489 or specialsales@sterlingpublishing.com.

Manufactured in China

Lot #:
2 4 6 8 10 9 7 5 3 1
09/18

sterlingpublishing.com

Cover and interior design by Heather Kelly
The artwork in this book was created digitally.

Mirabel's
Missing Valentines

written by Janet Lawler

illustrated by
Olivia Chin Mueller

STERLING CHILDREN'S BOOKS
New York

Mirabel was very shy.
She'd always been that way.
She trembled at the thought of
giving valentines away.

Despite her nerves, the night before,
she crafted works of art.

She signed the cards "From Mirabel."
On each, she drew a heart.

When morning came, she got up late—
she didn't want to go.
She dawdled over breakfast.
Her whole routine was slow.

She forced herself to leave for school
and hurried down the road,
not noticing as time went on
she had a lighter load.

A lonely lady looked inside
her empty mailbox twice.
But after Mirabel went by,
she smiled and thought, *How nice!*

Construction workers sweating
as they dug around a pole
laughed to find a sweet surprise
half-buried in the hole.

A busy papa waiting
for the light to change to *walk*
danced around in circles when
he heard his baby talk.

A jogger on her morning run
got stuck in gooey gum.
Something sparkled by her foot
that made her start to hum.

A garbage man enduring
yet another rotten smell
chuckled as he grabbed a scrap
before the scooper fell.

Then everybody heard a cry—

"I'VE LOST MY VALENTINES!!"

And so it dawned on each of them,
Perhaps this isn't mine.

They hurried up to Mirabel.
"Your cards have made us smile!"

"Thanks for sharing them with us,
if only for a while."

Mirabel was happy that
she'd brightened up their day.

Now she'd made a few new friends—
perhaps she'd be okay.

That afternoon at party time,
she joined in all the fun.

She traded cards with courage,
and she beamed when it was done.

Skipping home when school let out,
she paused atop the hill

and realized, to her delight,
her sack was fuller still.